This book belongs to

. . . .

. . . .

. . . .

GW Publishing
www.gwpublishing.com

To Sheila with love, a great friend and sister-in-law
– LS

In fond memory of my favourite father-in-law
– SJC

Text and Illustrations copyright © Linda Strachan and Sally J. Collins

www.lindastrachan.com

First published in paperback in Great Britain 2006
Reprinted 2014, 2016

The rights of Linda Strachan and Sally J. Collins to be identified
as the author and illustrator of this work have been asserted by them
in accordance with the Copyright, Designs and Patents Act 1988

Design - Veneta Hooper

Reprographics - GWP Graphics

Printed in China

Published by

GW Publishing
PO Box 15070
Dunblane,
FK15 5AN

Tel +44 (0) 1786 823278
www.gwpublishing.com

ISBN 09551564-2-4
978-09551564-2-7 ISBN-13

Greyfriars Bobby

By Linda Strachan

Illustrated by Sally J. Collins

The snow was thick and crisp as Alistair Dougall struggled to get his wagon through the wintry Edinburgh streets. Amidst the sacks of carrots, cabbages and winter kale he was taking to market was a large basket covered in a warm blanket. Inside the basket a small puppy squirmed and wriggled. Every now and then his daughter, Jean, would pick up the puppy and put him on her lap.

"I wish we could keep this one, Father, I like him best. He's so bright and alert."

"He'll make a good police dog then. Ye can get two pounds for a police dog," he told her.

Jean was wide-eyed at the thought. "Two pounds," she said in a whisper.

Constable John Gray, known to his friends as Auld Jock, was walking through the town with his son, Young Jock. He saw Alistair Dougall's wagon and waved him to stop.

"Did ye bring the dog, Alistair?" he shouted to the farmer. Alistair stopped the wagon and Jean handed the little dog down to Young Jock.

"He looks lively. What do you think?" Auld Jock asked his son.

"Aye Da, he looks feisty enough. Ouch!" Young Jock shook his finger where the puppy had nipped him. "His teeth are sharp enough, too."

"We'll be taking him then, Alistair," Auld Jock said with a grin and he paid the farmer the two pounds he had promised him.

"We're going to call him Bobby!" Young Jock told Jean.

"*Here comes Bobby, keekin doon the lobby!*" Jean sang the rhyme all the children called to the policemen when they saw them. "That's a fine name for a police dog."

Wee Bobby soon discovered that he liked being a police dog. He trotted along beside Auld Jock as they walked his beat, barking at anything he thought was suspicious. He loved to challenge the bigger dogs, bravely growling at them, even though he was half their size, but he rarely got into a fight because he knew Auld Jock wouldn't stand for it.

When the market was on there were farmers and fishwives and all sorts of stalls in the Grassmarket where you could buy almost anything you needed. The soldiers in their tartan trews and kilts came down from the barracks up in the Castle.

Auld Jock was well liked for his kind manner and his lively little dog and Bobby grew to love his master. He would always come when Jock called him. When they finished their shift they often went to the Coffee House where Mr Ramsay, the owner, gave Bobby a bowl of bread and milk, stew, or a bone from the soup pot.

When Auld Jock was going out on nightshift Bobby sat by the fire and watched him get ready. Jock pulled on his heavy dark coat and put on his belt, tucking in his rattle and making sure he had his whistle, notepad and pen. Knowing that it was almost time to leave, Bobby shook himself awake and eagerly picked up Jock's wooden baton, his tail wagging as he waited by the door for his master. Mrs Gray handed her husband his piece – a carefully wrapped sandwich – and his flask of hot tea. Picking up his hat, Jock opened the door and took the baton from Bobby, who raced down the stairs and out through Hall's Court into the High Street.

Greyfriars Kirkyard had to be checked once every hour during the night for thieves who might try to break into the houses that backed onto it. Some of the policemen were scared of going into the kirkyard after dark, frightened by tales of ghosts, but Auld Jock paid no heed to these stories. Bobby liked to chase the cats who inhabited the kirkyard at night, but he never strayed far from his master and a quick whistle always brought him back to the circle of light cast by Auld Jock's lantern.

A policeman's job meant spending long nights out in all weather and Auld Jock and Bobby frequently arrived home cold and soaking wet. Bobby would shake himself thoroughly and then settle down in front of the fire. But Auld Jock was not as strong as his wee dog. One day in October, when Bobby was about three years old, they were having dinner at the Coffee House as they often did.

Cough! Cough!

"That's a nasty cough you've got, Auld Jock," said Mr Ramsay.

"Och, it's nothing. It'll be gone in a day or two," Auld Jock told him. But the cough didn't go away, in fact it just got worse. Within a few weeks, Auld Jock was so ill that one morning he couldn't get up to go to work, so his wife called the doctor.

The doctor came and told him that he would not be able to go back to work for a while.

By New Year Jock was much worse. Bobby rarely left his side, sleeping close by his bed at night and lying beside him most of the day. Eventually Mrs Gray called in the doctor again, but he just shook his head.

"I'm sorry," he said sadly. "But there is nothing more I can do for him."

The next morning Auld Jock wouldn't wake up when Bobby jumped onto the bed. Mrs Gray felt sorry for the little dog, but she had no way to make him understand that his master was dead.

Auld Jock had passed away peacefully in his sleep.

On the day of Auld Jock's funeral Bobby walked along
the road with Young Jock and through the gates of
Greyfriars Kirkyard where he had been so many times
with his master on nightshift. He wasn't pleased when
Young Jock picked him up to carry him out of the
graveyard after the funeral was over. Bobby wanted
to stay beside the hole in the ground and the strange
wooden box where he knew his master was.

"Come on Bobby," Young Jock said. "It's time to go home."
Bobby wriggled and struggled all the way and when they
got home he scratched at the door and whined to be let out so
that he could go and find his master again. Mrs Gray and the
neighbours who had come to the house for the farewell tea
tried to coax him with treats but nothing worked.

As soon as the door was opened to let someone out Bobby was away. He ran as fast as he could but it was after sundown and the graveyard gates were locked. He tried to squeeze under the gates but he couldn't get in. He lay down and waited until the two policemen on night duty opened the gates to do their rounds and then Bobby slipped through like a shadow in the darkness.

He ran to the spot where Auld Jock had been buried and lay down on the soft mound of earth to wait for his master to tell him it was time to go home.

It was a cold wintry night and when it began to rain Bobby crept over to shelter under the table-shaped gravestone that stood next to Auld Jock's grave.

When James Brown, the gardener who looked after the kirkyard, came out of his house the following morning, he saw a scruffy little dog lying on the new grave.

"Get oot o here, ye wee tyke!" he shouted, waving his broom to scare Bobby away.

Bobby started barking but he refused to move from his master's grave.

James Brown shook his head. "You're a determined wee thing aren't ye? Wait a minute, you're Auld Jock's dog. Aye, that's who ye are, wee Bobby! Have ye been oot here all night?"

The gardener was sorry for the bedraggled little creature and went inside and brought Bobby a bowl of bread and milk. Bobby was starving and quickly polished it off, licking the bowl clean with his small pink tongue.

The gardener knew he was supposed to keep dogs out of the kirkyard but he didn't have the heart to send Bobby away. "I don't suppose it'll dae any harm," he muttered to himself.

So he left Bobby to settle down again on top of his master's grave and went about his business of clearing the paths and tidying up the graves.

At dinnertime Bobby waited to see if his master would be taking him to the Coffee House as usual. But when Auld Jock didn't come to take him, Bobby decided to go and see if his master was there already.

Mr Ramsay was surprised to see him. "Hello, Bobby," he said, stooping down to pat Bobby's head. "Sad to be without your master, are you?"

He went into the kitchen to tell his wife that wee Bobby was there. She came out with a bowl of stew and laid it down in the usual place. "You'll be needing a wee bit dinner, Bobby," she said with a sad smile.

When he was finished Bobby returned to keep vigil over his master's grave, loyally waiting for Auld Jock to take him on his rounds once more.

And that was how it was for the next few years. Bobby found he had many friends and he was a favourite with the local children. Mr Anderson the upholsterer and Mr Ritchie the tailor, who both had houses that backed onto the kirkyard, would offer Bobby a little food or shelter in the worst weather and always had a kind word for him.

Bobby slept most nights beside his master's grave, except when the weather was particularly bad and James Brown, the gardener, would open his door to let Bobby come in and sleep beside the fire. In the morning Bobby would run out and lie down once more on Auld Jock's grave.

It was around this time that the tradition began of firing a one o'clock gun from the battlements of Edinburgh Castle. It was a daily time check for the folk of Edinburgh, but wee Bobby recognised it too, and when he heard the gun he knew it was time for his meal. He was becoming famous and the children would stand outside the kirkyard to wait for him.

"Look, there he is!" they shouted, and everyone would stop to watch as Bobby ran out of the gates and headed straight for the Coffee House.

One day the Coffee House got a new owner, Mr Traill.
When he heard about Bobby he was delighted to welcome
the famous wee dog every day for his dinner.

Mr Traill's daughter, Elizabeth, was particularly fond of Bobby and one
day as she watched him devour a bowl of stew, she turned to her father.

"I think he should have his own bowl, Father," she said.

Mr Traill liked the wee dog, so the next day he bought a dish for Bobby
and had his name written on it.

A few years later there was a knock on Mr Traill's door. There stood two constables on their beat.

"You've no paid the money for your dog's licence, Mr Traill," the constable said.

"What dog?" Mr Traill scowled at him. "I've no got a dog."

The constable frowned. "Everybody knows you have a dog, Mr Traill. I've seen it come in here ma sel. You feed it, so ye can't tell me you've no got a dog."

Mr Traill laughed. "You must mean Bobby. You know fine weel he's no my dog. He's Auld Jock's dog."

The constable turned red and glowered at him. "Auld Jock's been dead for years and if you don't pay the licence it'll be the courts you'll hear from next."

If Bobby didn't have a licence his life would be in danger because stray dogs were caught by the dogcatchers and put down. No one wanted that to happen to Bobby.

The Lord Provost of Edinburgh at the time was William Chambers. He loved dogs and when he heard about Bobby he asked to have him brought to his house, so that he could meet the famous wee dog.

The children were worried that Bobby didn't have a licence so they went with him to meet the Lord Provost.

"I've heard all about you, Bobby," Mr Chambers said, scratching Bobby behind the ears. "And I think that as you live in the kirkyard which belongs to the town council, then it is only fair that the town council should pay your licence fee. I shall have a collar made for you, with a fine brass name plate on it, for everybody to see."

Bobby barked gently and licked the man's hand.

Mr Chamber's decision was reported in newspapers far and wide, where they told the story of the faithful wee dog who had stayed by his master's grave for many years. Artists came and drew his portrait, photographers and journalists took his picture and wrote articles about the famous 'Greyfriars Bobby' as he was now becoming known. But Bobby took little notice of all this and continued to lie on his master's grave and trot round to the Traill's Coffee House for his lunch at one o'clock as usual.

As the years went by and Bobby grew older, he liked
to spend some of the coldest nights at the fireside with
Elizabeth Traill and her family.

One January night when he was a very old dog,
almost sixteen years old . . .

. . . Bobby curled up beside the fire and drifted
away peacefully into his final sleep.

Bobby had stayed by his master's grave for many years, but it was against the law to bury dogs in the graveyard. Mr Traill and some of his friends decided to bury Bobby secretly in the Greyfriars Kirkyard because they couldn't bear to think of Bobby being separated from his beloved master.

And there he rests to this day.

A statue of Bobby stands proudly, close to the entrance to Greyfriars Kirkyard at the top of Candlemaker's Row in Edinburgh. It watches over the path where Bobby walked every day for so many years from the kirkyard to the Coffee House.